Write your letter to Santa…

Inside the pocket you will find two sheets
of writing paper and an envelope.

Take out the writing paper and write your
address at the top. Then write your Christmas wish-list
in the spaces.

When you have finished your list, don't forget to write
your name at the bottom.

Then put the letter in the envelope and copy Santa's address
from the envelope opposite.

You can post your letter up the chimney or in the post box
and it will find its way to Santa.

Merry Christmas!

This edition published by Parragon in 2012
Parragon
Chartist House
15–17 Trim Street
Bath BA1 1HA, UK
www.parragon.com

ISBN 978-1-4454-4320-1

Printed in China

A Letter to
Santa

PaRRagon

Bath · New York · Singapore · Hong Kong · Cologne · Delhi
Melbourne · Amsterdam · Johannesburg · Shenzhen

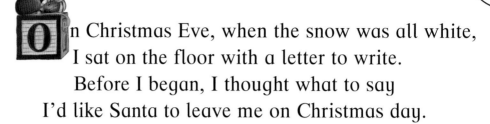

On Christmas Eve, when the snow was all white,
I sat on the floor with a letter to write.
Before I began, I thought what to say
I'd like Santa to leave me on Christmas day.

Dear Santa,

(I neatly wrote)
I hope you are well
when you read this note.
I'm sure you have noticed
that I have been good,
just as my mummy
told me I should.
So if it's alright,
for Christmas I'd like –
a book or a train set
or maybe a bike.

Then when I'd finished, I printed my name,
and added kisses again and again.

Across to the fireplace I boldly went,
and up the chimney my letter was sent.
For that is the place, I'm sure you will know,
that letters to Santa should always go.
Just how they get there, I don't understand,
but that is the way to Santa's cold land.

That winter's night when the world was asleep,
I snuggled in bed – not a sound, not a peep –
thinking of Santa and the toys he would bring,
and the fun I would have on Christmas morning.
When, all of a sudden, where could I be?
Out in the snow in a strange country!

Next to a cabin in the deep crispy snow,
I shiver with cold as I peer in the window.
It's Santa's workshop! I must creep inside.
No one will see me if I'm careful to hide.
Sssh! I must be quiet as I tiptoe in,
to see where our Christmas toys all begin.

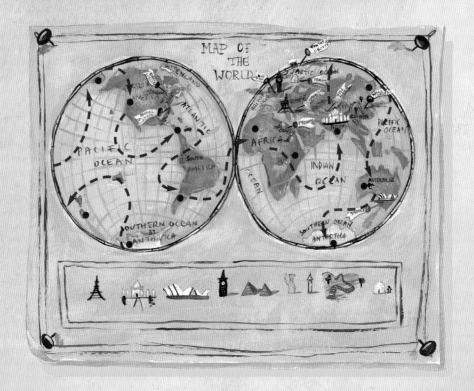

I can see Santa reading letters galore.
Hey, he's got mine, by his feet, on the floor!
A map of the world is pinned to the wall,
showing Santa the way to the homes of us all,
with rooftop instructions so there is no doubt,
that any small child is ever left out.

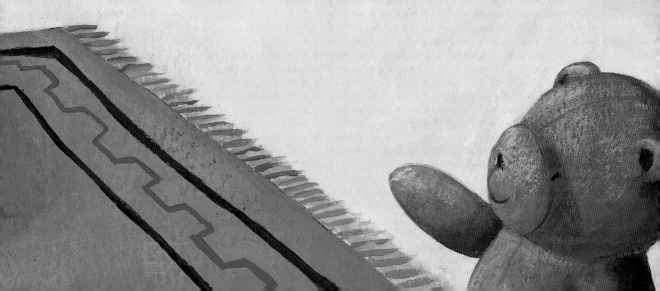

Just see how busy all Santa's elves are:
One's making a doll's house, one a toy car;
another elf's painting a wonderful train,

and this elf is putting the wings on a plane.
Look at that little elf riding a bike,
It's just like the one I said I would like.

This must be the room where presents are packed.
They're measured for size, then carefully wrapped.
Tied up with ribbons and finished with bows,
each with a name tag so Santa Claus knows.
Wherever you look there's bustle and scurry.
Everyone seems in a terrible hurry.

Here are the elves who help Santa get dressed.
There's Santa's coat and hat, all neatly pressed.
And there are his boots getting a shine.
They look so smart, I wish they were mine.
I think this room is as good as the rest,
for it's the place that makes Santa look best.

Back in the workshop, the parcel track halts.
It seems there's a problem with one of its bolts.
The elves are worried – there's trouble in the air.
But here comes Santa to make the repair.
In no time at all, parcels speed on their way,
out to the stables and onto the sleigh.

Outside the stable, the reindeer wait.
I count them all up and, yes, there are eight!
Their hooves are polished, their bells burnished bright,
as elves brush and groom them in the moonlight.
Their harnesses gleam, their coats all shine.
Now the reindeer are restless, as it's almost time!

The sleigh is now packed and the reindeer ready.
Santa at the reins cries, "Away now, go steady!"
High over clouds and hills they fly,
galloping onwards across the sky.
Soon, beneath them, rooftops they see
where inside asleep are children like me!

When I wake up, it's Christmas Day,
and just like my dream, Santa's been! Hooray!
My stocking is filled up with candy cane,
And I'm sure in that parcel there must be a train.
Great! There's a bicycle propped by my bed.
My letter to Santa must have been read!